the CRiTTeR club

Marion Strikes a Pose

by Callie Barkley ♥ illustrated by Marsha Riti

LITTLE SIMON
New York London Toronto Sydney New Delhi

LITTLE SIMON

An imprint of Simon & Schuster Children's Publishing Division • 1230 Avenue of the Americas, New York, New York 10020 • First Little Simon edition July 2014 • Copyright © 2014 by Simon & Schuster, Inc. All rights reserved, including the right of reproduction in whole or in part in any form. LITTLE SIMON is a registered trademark of Simon & Schuster, Inc., and associated colophon is a trademark of Simon & Schuster, Inc. For information about special discounts for bulk purchases, please contact Simon & Schuster Special Sales at 1-866-506-1949 or business@simonandschuster.com. The Simon & Schuster Speakers Bureau can bring authors to your live event. For more information or to book an event contact the Simon & Schuster Speakers Bureau at 1-866-248-3049 or visit our website at www.simonspeakers.com. Designed by Laura Roode. The text of this book was set in ITC Stone Informal Std.
Manufactured in the United States of America 0416 MTN   6 8 10 9 7 5
Library of Congress Cataloging-in-Publication Data
Barkley, Callie. Marion strikes a pose / by Callie Barkley ; illustrated by Marsha Riti. — First edition. pages cm. — (The Critter Club ; #8) Summary: While her friends in the Critter Club babysit frogs, second-grader Marion enters a fashion design contest. [1. Fashion design—Fiction. 2. Contests—Fiction.] I. Riti, Marsha, illustrator. II. Title. PZ7.B250585Mar 2014 [Fic]—dc23 2013024708
ISBN 978-1-4424-9529-6 (hc)
ISBN 978-1-4424-9528-9 (pbk)
ISBN 978-1-4424-9530-2 (eBook)

Table of Contents

Chapter 1

Ready, Set, Style!

Marion walked in the front door of Santa Vista Elementary School. In her head, she was going through her morning checklist: *Homework folder? Check. Lunch box? Check. Sneakers for gym? Check.*

Marion felt ready for the day.

She followed other kids into the auditorium for the morning

assembly, which they had every Friday. The seats were filling up. Marion headed for the rows assigned to the second-grade classes. She spotted an empty seat next to her three best friends, Amy, Liz, and Ellie.

Walking toward that row, Marion passed a group of fourth

graders. "I love your skirt, Marion!" said a girl named Emily as Marion went by.

"Thanks!" Marion replied. She had spent a lot of time last night planning her outfit for today. She added one more item to her check-list. *Cool outfit? Check!* Marion loved picking out her outfits for

school. And for play dates and for parties. And for riding her horse, Coco. For everything, really!

"Hi, Marion!" said Amy as she sat down. Farther down the row, Ellie and Liz waved.

"Attention, students!" Mrs. Young,

the principal, spoke into the microphone at the front of the auditorium.
All the kids quieted down. "I have
some announcements. But
first, we have a special
guest. Her name is
Hannah Lewis. She
is the owner of The
Closet, a store here
in Santa Vista."

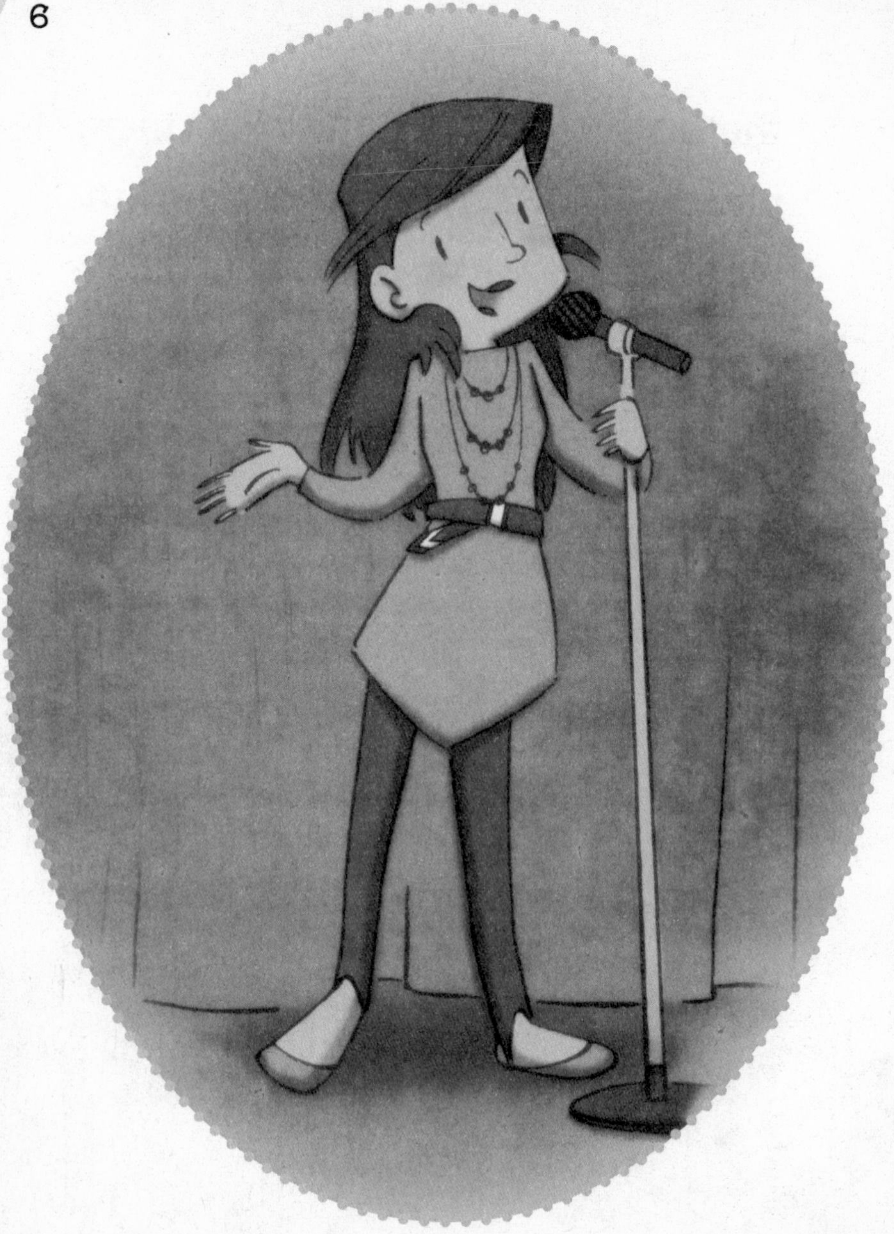

The students clapped.

Marion gasped. *The Closet!* It was her absolute favorite clothing store.

Marion sat up straight in her seat as Hannah Lewis walked up to the microphone. Marion loved Hannah's outfit— an extra-long top with a leather belt, black leggings, and ballet flats. Plus she had on some cool beaded necklaces.

"Good morning, everyone," said Hannah. "Thank you, Mrs. Young, for letting me come today. I want to announce that we will be having a special fashion show at The Closet in a few weeks."

A fashion show, Marion thought. *How fun!*

"The purpose of the show is to raise money for a charity," said

Hannah. "It provides free clothing to children who need it, so it's a very good cause. We hope the fashion show will get lots of people to come shopping at our store that day. All the money we earn will go to the charity."

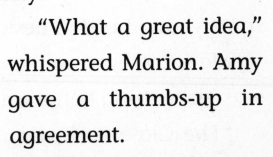

"What a great idea," whispered Marion. Amy gave a thumbs-up in agreement.

"But I need *your* help,"

Hannah went on. "Our store is a *kids'* clothing store. And I was thinking: Who knows best what kids like to wear? Kids! So I am looking for some young fashion designers."

Marion's eyes went wide. This was just getting better and better!

"The Closet is having a styling contest," Hannah explained. "To enter, you style an outfit—head to toe. I will pick one winning look from each grade. Those will be the outfits in our fashion show!"

Now Marion was so excited she could hardly sit still!

"Contest entries are due a week from Monday," Hannah went on. "I have flyers here with all the rules. If you are interested, please come up to get one."

Marion jumped out of her seat, ready to get a flyer.

Seeing Marion, Hannah laughed. *"After* assembly," she added. "But I like your enthusiasm."

Marion sat back down, too excited to even be embarrassed. She felt as if this contest had been made just for her.

I have to win! she thought. *I just have to!*

Chapter 2

Froggy Fashion Show

After school, the girls met at The Critter Club. That was the animal shelter they had started in their friend Ms. Sullivan's empty barn. At the club, they took care of stray and hurt animals and tried to find homes for them.

They also did a lot of pet sitting. Right now at The Critter Club they

were taking care of some frogs for a family that was on vacation. It was Liz and Marion's turn to check on the frogs, but Amy and Ellie had come, too. It was fun to all be there together.

Always organized, Marion pulled the frog feeding schedule

from her backpack. "I guess it's my day to feed them," she said. "But, do you want to do it, Liz?"

"Yes!" Liz cried excitedly. For Liz, the more unusual the animal, the better. Turtles, snakes, spiders—she loved them all.

Marion shivered. The frogs were not exactly *her* favorite Critter Club guests. They looked so slimy. And they ate bugs. Yuck!

While Liz fed the frogs, Marion pulled the contest flyer out of her backpack. She hadn't stopped thinking about it since assembly.

The Closet's Styling Contest!

Style a head-to-toe outfit for a girl or boy.

Use your own clothes or come "shop" at The Closet to borrow clothes for your outfit design!

"Are you going to enter?" Marion asked her friends.

Amy shook her head no. "Maybe if it was a writing contest," she said with a smile.

Liz also shook her head. "I don't know how to *design* an outfit. Mine just kind of happen."

"What about you, Ellie?" Marion asked. Ellie loved dressing up. Ellie twirled around and then curtsied. "I'd rather be *on* the stage than styling *back*stage." she replied.

The girls all laughed. That was Ellie, all right! She loved being in the spotlight.

"Well, I have a favor to ask of you guys," Marion said. "I stopped

at home and picked out an outfit for each of you from my closet.
You know, to get my styling ideas
started."

Marion pulled out the clothes
she'd brought. "I thought we could
play Fashion Show. Right here in
the barn!"

Marion had brought a sparkly skirt and satin blouse for Ellie.

"Cuuuuute!" Ellie cooed. She rushed into a storage room to try them on. She was back in less than a minute.

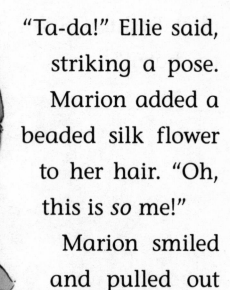

"Ta-da!" Ellie said, striking a pose. Marion added a beaded silk flower to her hair. "Oh, this is *so* me!"

Marion smiled and pulled out Amy's outfit. It

was a striped yellow T-shirt dress.

"Would you try it on?" Marion asked Amy. *"Please?"*

Amy didn't look so sure about the fashion show idea, but she agreed. She went off to change and came back, all smiles.

"This is *definitely* something I would wear," Amy said.

Finally, Marion had a colorful outfit for Liz: a bright green dress and rainbow-striped leggings.

Liz had just taken the lid off the frog tank to feed the frogs, but she

glanced over. When she saw the outfit, she clapped happily. "I can't wait to try that on! You really know our styles!"

"Thanks, Liz." Marion said. "That's so nice to—EEEEEK!"

Marion shrieked as a frog jumped out of the tank.

The frog landed on the table.

"I'll get it!" said Amy. "Oh, wait! We're not supposed to touch them." Amy grabbed a butterfly net. She tried to catch the frog but it quickly hopped away. "Hey, come back here!" she cried.

The frog hopped onto the outfit Marion had brought for Liz.

"Shoo! Shoo!" Marion cried. The slimy frog was hopping all over the clothes! "Somebody get it off!"

Finally, Amy scooped up the frog in the net. She gently put it back into the frog tank. Marion took a deep breath. Liz, Amy, and Ellie turned to look at her.

Then all four girls burst out laughing.

"You know, Marion," said Liz, "frogs are really cool in lots of ways."

Amy nodded. "My mom is going to come next week. She can teach us more about them."

Amy's mom, Dr. Melanie Purvis, was a veterinarian. She often helped the girls care for the animals at The

Critter Club. "Who knows? Maybe you'll even learn to like them."

Marion smiled and didn't say anything. *I wouldn't count on that!* she thought.

A Wrinkle in the Plan

"What a great idea!" said Liz. She was looking at the stack of cards Marion had made over the weekend. Each one had a photo of an item of clothing Marion owned.

"I call them style cards," Marion said as Liz handed them back. "I can carry them around and flip through them to get design ideas."

It was Monday and their class was in the art room. Liz and Marion sat across from each other at one end of a long table. Today they were painting with watercolors.

Marion had carefully painted a few lines, but most of her paper was empty. She didn't love painting.

Paintbrushes didn't have erasers. What if she messed up?

Next to Marion, a girl named Olivia leaned over. "Marion," she said, "could *I* look at those?" She pointed at the stack of style cards.

"Sure!" Marion replied. She handed the cards to Olivia.

Olivia studied them carefully, looking very interested. "You always wear the coolest outfits," she told Marion.

Marion smiled. "Thanks!" she exclaimed.

Olivia nodded and went back to flipping through the cards.

Marion was surprised by the compliment. She had never really noticed Olivia's taste in clothes before. Today Olivia was wearing a purple sweater with a crooked heart on it, black jeans, and purple high-top sneakers. It seemed like their styles were really different.

Olivia passed the cards back. "Thanks for letting me

look," she said, and gave Marion a friendly smile. Marion smiled back.

"Could I ask you a favor?" Olivia asked her.

Marion nodded. "Sure."

"Well, I was wondering . . ." Olivia began. She looked unsure of her words. "Could you maybe, I

don't know, give *me* some fashion tips sometime?"

Marion was so flattered. She and Olivia were friendly, but they didn't know each other super well. *She must* really *like my fashion sense to ask me for advice*, Marion thought.

Marion smiled. "Sure!" she told Olivia.

"Thanks!" Olivia exclaimed happily. "Maybe now I'll have a shot at winning."

Marion was confused. "Winning?" she asked.

Olivia nodded.

"Winning the styling contest," Olivia explained. "I'm entering, too."

"Oh." It was all Marion could think of to say. But her mind was racing. She and Olivia were both in second grade. Hannah would choose only one winning look from

each grade. So if Olivia was entering, and Marion was entering, that
meant . . .

Olivia was her competition.

And Marion had just agreed to
help her win.

Chapter 4

Style School

Marion laughed, looking down at her Saturday breakfast. Her mom had made it look like a mouse in a sleeping bag. The mouse had a banana-slice head, chocolate-chip eyes, and two blueberry ears. The sleeping bag was a folded pancake. There was even a pillow—a toast rectangle—under the mouse's head.

Marion hurried to finish her breakfast before Olivia came over. The girls were getting to be good friends. Already Olivia had been over three times that week.

At first Marion wasn't sure about helping Olivia. But she quickly changed her mind. After all, she was just giving Olivia fashion tips—not styling her outfit *for* her.

So on Tuesday, Olivia came over after school. Together the girls played mix-and-match design with all of Marion's style cards.

"Don't be afraid to mix patterns and fabrics," Marion advised. "A denim jacket looks great with a silky striped skirt."

On Wednesday, the girls played dress-up with Marion's party clothes. Olivia didn't even mind that Gabby, Marion's little sister, wanted to play, too. She had a little

brother about the same age.

"Make sure *you* like your outfit," Marion said, sharing another tip. "Clothes look better if you feel good wearing them."

On Thursday, the two of them talked about accessories: scarves, belts, and shoes.

"You know, one fun accessory can make a whole outfit better!" Marion pointed out.

Marion liked getting to know Olivia. Olivia was really nice. She liked animals. And she cared about the charity that The Closet was raising money for. Olivia reminded Marion that the contest wasn't all about winning; it was also about helping people.

By Saturday, Marion not only really liked Olivia, she also wanted Olivia to do well in the contest.

It was a nice day, so the girls sat

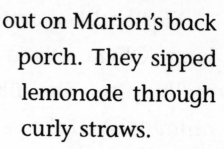

out on Marion's back porch. They sipped lemonade through curly straws.

"Okay, here it is," said Marion. "This is my big fashion tip. Pick one part of your design— either the shoes, or the pants, or the

top, or an accessory. Pick one part
and do something . . . unexpected!
Make it unique."

Olivia nodded. "That makes

sense," she said. "So, nothing *too* crazy. But something that will make our outfits stand out in the contest." She pulled her curly straw out of her glass. "Like this straw," she said with a giggle. "You could use it in an outfit as a—"

"Cool hair accessory!" Marion suggested.

Olivia's jaw dropped. "That's what I was going to say!"

Marion laughed. "Great minds think alike," she said.

Frog Facts

Later that afternoon, Marion was outside The Critter Club playing fetch with Ms. Sullivan's dog, Rufus. She threw a stick across Ms. Sullivan's backyard. "Go get it!" she said.

Rufus bounded after the stick. He was getting so big! Marion could remember when she'd first met Rufus. He'd gotten lost one day and the girls helped Ms. Sullivan find him.

Rufus brought the stick back. He dropped it at Marion's feet. It was covered in doggy slobber.

"Ew, Rufus," Marion said with a laugh.

"Ma-ri-on!" Amy called from the barn door. "My mom's here."

Amy's mom had come to teach the girls more about frogs. Ellie and Liz were already inside.

Marion gave Rufus a good-bye pat
and headed for the barn.

Dr. Purvis was standing by the
frog tank. Ellie, Liz, and Amy were
gathered around.

"Hi, Marion," Dr. Purvis said. "I

want to show you girls how to clean out the frog tank. But first, how about I share some of my favorite frog facts?"

"Okay!" said the girls together.

"Here's one," said Dr. Purvis. "You know how we call a group of birds a *flock*? Well, we call a group of frogs . . . an *army*."

The girls laughed.

"An army of frogs," said Marion. "Oh no. I'm getting a picture in my mind. It's totally terrifying!"

"Wait," said Amy. "Listen to this one. Mom, tell them the one about the skin."

Dr. Purvis smiled. "Yes, well, most frogs shed their skin about once a week."

Liz looked puzzled. "Once a week?" she said. "But we've had these frogs for a week." She looked into the frog tank. "Why aren't there any old frog skins anywhere?"

"Good question, Liz," Dr. Purvis said. "You don't see the old skins because the frogs *eat* them."

"Coooool!" said Liz.

"Whoa," said Ellie.

"Yikes!" said Marion. They ate bugs *and* their own skin? She was mostly grossed out. But one part of it was cool: The frogs weren't letting anything go to waste.

"I have a question," said Ellie. "Why can't we touch them?"

"Because frog skin is thin and sensitive," Dr. Purvis explained. "It's designed to let in air and water—and whatever else it touches. Even right after we wash our hands, we still usually have stuff on them—like oils or soap residue. If we touch the frogs, then those things could get inside

the frog's body and make it sick. That wouldn't be good."

Hmm. That is pretty interesting, Marion thought. She leaned down and peered into the tank. One of the frogs seemed to be staring back at her.

She pretended the frog could read her mind. *I don't want to pick you up,* she thought. *And you don't want me to pick you up.*

Somehow, knowing that made Marion like the frogs better. It was like they understood one another.

chapter 6

Decisions, Decisions

The big day had come.

Shopping day!

Marion's mom had driven her to The Closet so she could borrow clothing, as the flyer said. She was picking out the actual clothes that would make up her outfit. Then, at school tomorrow, she would meet with Hannah to present the outfit.

"I'll be right over there, looking at shoes for Gabby," Marion's mom said. "Call me if you need me."

Marion was happy to browse on her own. In fact, she was in heaven. Marion looked down at her notebook. It was open to her outfit sketch.

She was most proud of the scarf
idea she'd had. She was hoping to
find an extra-large patterned scarf
at The Closet. She wanted to tie it
over her basic pieces. It would be an
unexpected touch!

Already, Marion had found a
simple blue skirt and a matching
top. They were perfect for the base

layer. "Now where are the scarves?" Marion wondered.

Looking around for a salesperson to ask, she passed the fitting rooms. One of the doors opened. Out stepped . . . Olivia!

"Marion!" she cried.

"Hi, Olivia!" said Marion. "It's so funny that we're here at the same time." She looked down at what Olivia had on: a denim jacket with ruffles, a flowing green skirt, tights, and low brown boots. "Is this your design?" Marion asked. "I love it! It looks great!"

Olivia scrunched up her face.

"Really?" she said. "I'm not sure about it. Actually, I have another one in here. I think it's better than this one." Olivia's face brightened. "Can I show you? You can tell me which one *you* like better."

"Okay!" Marion replied.

Olivia went back into the fitting room. Meanwhile, Marion scanned the racks. She spotted some scarves on a shelf and headed over to check them out.

Behind her, Marion heard the fitting-room door open and then Olivia's voice. "So what do you think of this one?"

Marion turned. Her eyes took in Olivia's outfit, head to toe. Marion felt something like a knot twisting in her stomach.

Olivia was wearing slim purple pants and a sleeveless shirt. Over the top, tied to look like a dress, she had on *an extra-large flower print scarf.*

Marion could not believe it! Olivia's scarf looked like it had come straight out of Marion's notebook.

Marion thought the outfit was amazing. She *loved* it. She opened her mouth to say so. But she didn't want to say so. Because if that was Olivia's design, what would Marion do? Their outfits couldn't be so similar!

"It's nice," Marion said. "But you know what? The first outfit was better. I'd go with that other one."

As soon as the words were out of her mouth, Marion wished she could take them back.

A Strange Feeling

In the school auditorium, Marion was showing her outfit design to Hannah. She struggled to get the scarf tied the right way. Each knot she made just came untied.

Marion looked up. In the back of the auditorium, Olivia stood in the doorway. She pointed at Marion's scarf. "There it is!" Olivia cried. "Get it!"

Olivia stepped aside, and Marion saw it: an army of huge frogs. They were hopping two by two down the auditorium aisle. They were headed right for Marion!

Marion woke with a start.

Morning sunlight shone through her curtains. She sighed with relief. It was just a dream. A terrible, terrible dream.

But as Marion rubbed her eyes, a certain feeling in her stomach came back. What was it? Then Marion realized—she felt guilty. She had lied and convinced Olivia to choose the first outfit.

Then, after Olivia had left the store, Marion had gone ahead with her design. She had chosen the blue

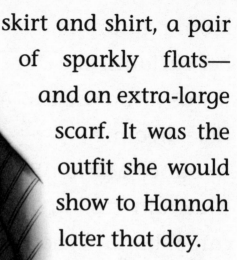

skirt and shirt, a pair of sparkly flats—and an extra-large scarf. It was the outfit she would show to Hannah later that day.

At least I didn't get the exact same scarf Olivia picked out, Marion thought, trying to make it seem less terrible. *Is it really such a big deal?*

But deep down, Marion knew it was. She had lied because she

wanted to win so badly.

Marion jumped out of bed. She had to get to school and find Olivia. She had to tell her the truth.

The Closet

Chapter 8

Marion Makes It Work

The clock outside the auditorium read 3:42. School was dismissed. The buses were gone. The pickup circle was empty.

The only students left at school were the ones who wanted to enter the styling contest. There were three other second graders, plus about ten kids from other grades.

But Olivia wasn't there. She hadn't been in school at all that day, so Marion hadn't had a chance to talk to her.

Marion was next in line to have her meeting with Hannah.

What am I going to do? Marion

READ BOOKS! It's Cool!

The Closet

wondered. Her heart beat faster. In a shopping bag, she had the clothes from The Closet. But Marion didn't feel good about them. *I want to win. But then, what if I do win? I won't feel proud or excited.*

The auditorium door opened. Hannah poked her head out and called, "Next!" She looked at Marion with a smile.

Marion took a deep breath as she walked in through the door.

At the foot of the stage, there was a mannequin the size of Marion. "Your name is Marion Ballard?" Hannah asked as she checked her clipboard. "And you're in second grade?"

Marion nodded.

"Great," said Hannah. "So, why don't I help you dress this

mannequin with the outfit you've put together. Then I'll have a few questions for you. Okay?"

"Sure," said Marion. She pulled out the blue skirt and the blue shirt. Hannah helped her wriggle the clothes onto the mannequin.

Then Marion pulled out the scarf.

"And where does this fit into your design?" Hannah asked.

"That goes . . ." Marion began. She froze. She couldn't do it. She just couldn't use the scarf the way she—and Olivia—had pictured it. It didn't feel right.

But she had to use the scarf. Otherwise, her outfit was too plain.

Thinking quickly, Marion held one end of the scarf. She twirled it around until it was twisted up, long and thin.

She wrapped it around the mannequin's waist like a belt and tied it
in a large bow at the right hip.

Marion stepped back to look at
it. It wasn't as good as her original
scarf idea. But it wasn't bad.

"Interesting," Hannah said, admiring the outfit. "That's an unexpected touch."

Marion smiled for the first time that day.

Chapter 9

The Moment of Truth

The rest of the meeting was a blur. Hannah asked Marion why she was entering the contest and a few other questions. Before Marion knew it, she was walking out of the auditorium.

As she opened the door, she saw Olivia waiting in line. "You're here!" Marion said. "But . . . where

have you been? Why weren't you in school today?"

Olivia wiped at her nose with a tissue. "My allergies were really bad this morning," she said. "My dad said I should stay home and rest." She held up a bag. "But I'm ready with my outfit. I can't wait for my turn to go in!"

Marion looked down at the floor. "Olivia, about your outfit," she began. This was going to be hard. Marion knew she had to tell Olivia the truth. "I lied to you yesterday. I said I liked your first outfit better, but really I *loved* your second outfit."

The Closet

Olivia looked confused. "You did?" she asked.

Marion nodded and explained everything—how they had had the same scarf idea, and how

Marion hadn't wanted to change her design. "I should have told you. We could have talked it over." She looked Olivia in the eye. "I'm sorry."

Olivia smiled. "That's okay, Marion," she said. "Because you know what? I'm not going to use

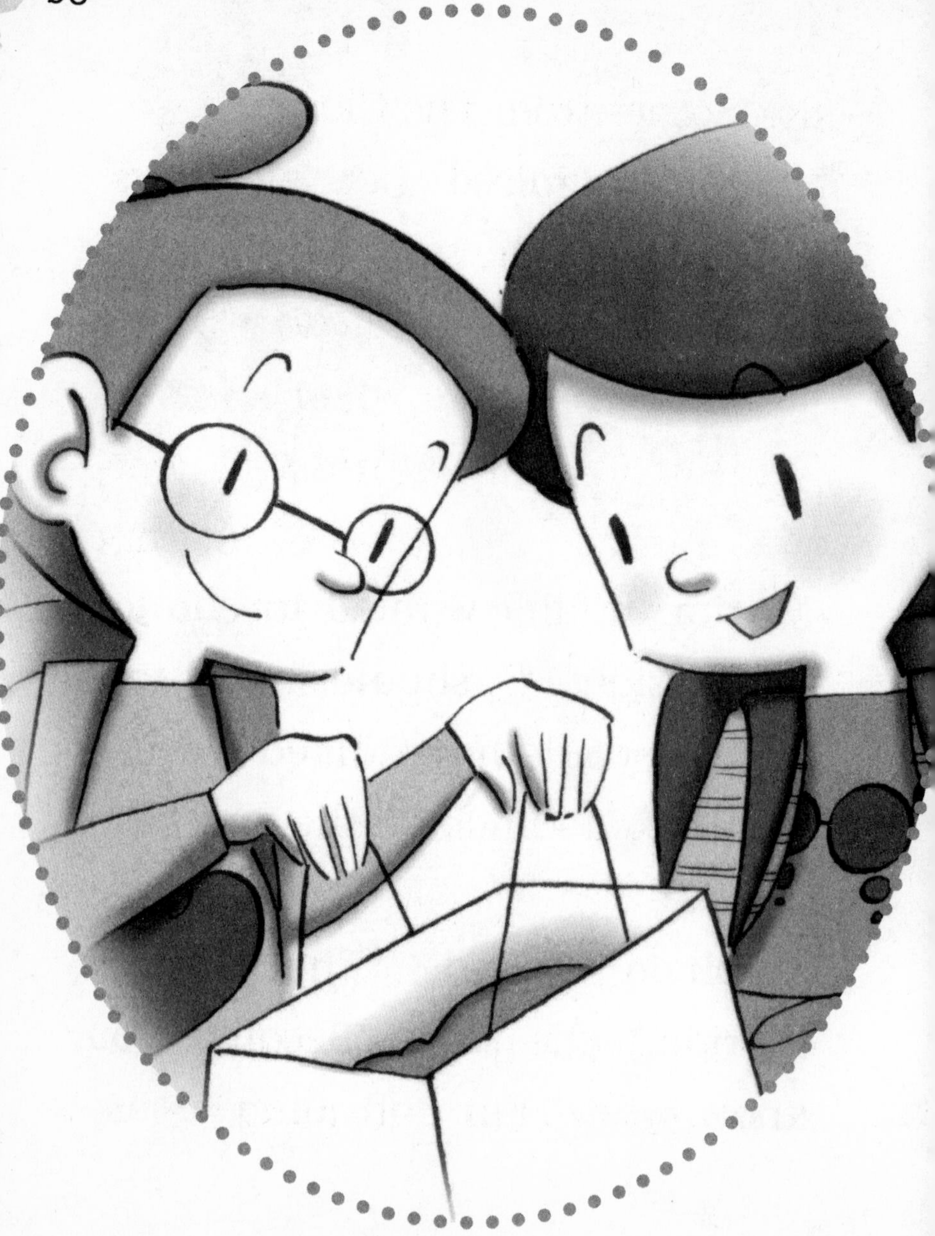

the clothes from The Closet."

Marion raised her eyebrows. "You're not?" she said.

Olivia shook her head. "See, I realized something when I was at home today," she started. "I realized that . . . I do kind of like my own style. I mean, I learned a lot from you, and your style is amazing. But it's just not mine."

Olivia opened her bag so Marion could peek in. "So this is my outfit: my high-top sneakers, a skirt that is so much fun to twirl around in, and my favorite

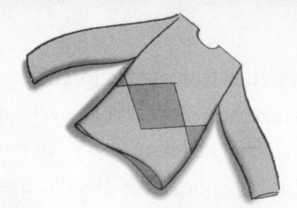

sweater. My grandma gave it to me. It's something I would feel good wearing."

Marion smiled a huge smile. "I love it!" she said. And she really meant it.

She waited in line with Olivia, then wished her good luck when Hannah called her in. "I'll wait out here until you're done," Marion said to Olivia.

Olivia nodded and gave her a thumbs-up as the auditorium door closed behind her.

Showtime!

A week later, Marion ran full speed into The Critter Club. "Hello?" she called, out of breath.

No one answered. "Amy? Liz? Ellie?" she said. It was time to feed the frogs. But the other girls hadn't arrived yet.

In one hand, Marion clutched a piece of paper. At last it had come

in the mail: a letter from Hannah Lewis with the list of contest winners. Marion sat down by the frog tank to wait. She looked inside. One of the frogs hopped right up to the glass.

"Oh, hello," Marion said to the

frog. She looked down at the letter. She looked back at the frog. Then she shrugged. She was dying to share the news with *someone*.

She held the letter up to the glass. "Look!" she exclaimed. "Look who won in second grade!"

Second-Grade Winners: Olivia Warren and Marion Ballard

The frog croaked.

"I know!" said Marion. "Isn't it great? I'm so excited!"

The frog didn't say anything else, so Marion went on. "I can't decide which is better. Winning, or winning *with* Olivia!"

There was no answer from the frog tank.

"And Hannah Lewis called me just now. She said she loved both of our designs. She said they were *both* so stylish and so different."

Marion was sure the frog was listening to every word she said.

"And here's maybe the best part: Hannah said if we want to, we can model our outfits in the fashion show! That's right. We can be *in* the show! Can you believe it?"

The frog was quiet. Marion

was all out of news. She sat for a
moment, just looking at the frog.
She leaned in closer to the glass.

"You know what?" whispered
Marion. "You are a very good

listener." She looked around. She felt a tiny bit silly talking to a frog. Then she added, "And you guys are *actually* pretty cool."

One week later, Marion was backstage at The Closet's fashion show. She peeked out at the audience from behind the curtain. The seats were filled and loud music played. Everyone clapped as the contest winners took turns walking the runway, showing off their outfit designs.

"Marion, you're next," Hannah

whispered behind her. "Ready . . . and go!"

Marion took a deep breath and stepped out onto the runway. She felt so proud to show off the outfit she had styled. She was even prouder of the hard decision she had made to

change her design. In the end, she loved the way the outfit turned out.

By the sound of the audience's applause, they liked it, too!

At the end of the narrow stage, Marion struck a pose. She could see her friends and family cheering loudly for her.

Marion turned and began her walk off stage. As she did, she passed Olivia on her way down the runway in her own winning outfit.

Marion put her hand up for a high five. The friends' hands met in the air with a loud clap.

Then, as Marion walked on, she smiled a huge smile, listening to the crowd cheer for her friend.

Read on for a sneak peek at
the next Critter Club book:

#9

Amy's Very
Merry Christmas

At her mom's vet clinic, Amy Purvis peeked into the guinea pigs' cage. She had just hung a new toy from its top. *Will they figure out how to play with it?* Amy wondered.

Snowy, the white guinea pig, tried it out first. He sniffed at the jingle bell dangling at the end of a silver velvet ribbon. *Jingle.* The bell rang softly. Snowy darted away and hid inside a tissue box.

His brother, Alfie, came over next. He nudged the bell with his paw. *Jingle-jingle!*

Before long, the two guinea pigs were taking turns batting at the bell.

Amy smiled as she watched them play. "Happy holidays, guys!"

It was a week before Christmas. Snowy and Alfie had been staying at the vet clinic for a few days. Their owner had brought them in because they seemed sick. They hadn't been eating or moving around much. But Amy's mom, Dr. Melanie Purvis, had known exactly what to do.

"Look at them now!" Amy's mom said, walking up behind Amy. "See? They just weren't getting enough vitamin C before. It's a common problem for guinea pigs." Dr. Purvis had fed the guinea pigs lots of oranges and kiwi fruit. "They're just about well enough to go home."

Amy gave a happy clap. "Yay! They'll be home in time for the holidays!" she said.

Amy loved animals, so she also loved helping out at her mom's clinic. It was in the building right next door to Amy's house, where she lived with her mom. On some weekdays, after school, Amy brought her homework over to the clinic. She sat at the front desk, did her reading and math, then helped with chores.

Today she cleaned out cages, refilled water bowls, and took two dogs for walks. But making the toy for Snowy and Alfie had definitely been the most fun.

"Mom," said Amy. "I just decided: I'm going to make a present for each animal at the clinic."

Dr. Purvis gave Amy a hug. "I think that's very nice of you," she said. "Maybe your Critter Club friends would like to help?"

"Great idea!" said Amy. She and her best friends, Marion, Liz, and Ellie, ran an animal shelter called The Critter Club. The club was in their friend Ms. Sullivan's barn. Together, the girls had helped lots of stray animals in

Santa Vista find new homes.

Right now, the club didn't have any animal guests. So it was a perfect time for the girls to find some other critters to help.

The animals at the clinic need some holiday cheer, Amy decided. *This is definitely a job for The Critter Club!*

If you like the CRITTER club you'll love HE!Di HECKELBECK

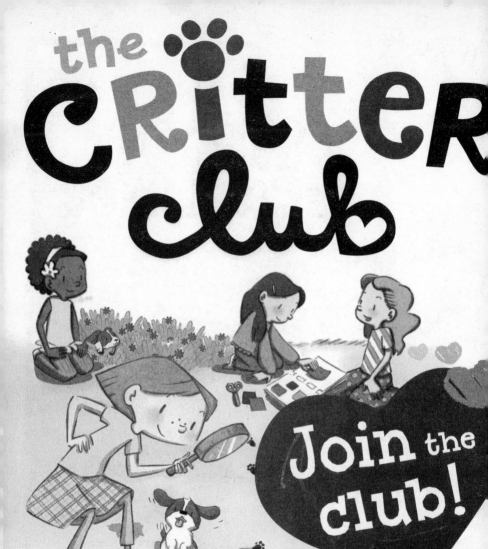

Join the club!